P9-EMH-005

MAGNIFICENT
HOMESPUN BROWN

Tilbury House Publishers • www.tilburyhouse.com • Text © 2020 by Samara Cole Doyon • Illustrations © 2020 by Kaylani Juanita
All rights reserved. No part of this publication may be reproduced or transmitted in any form or by any means, electronic or
mechanical, including photocopying, recording, or any information storage or retrieval system, without permission in writing
from the publisher. • Hardcover ISBN 978-0-88448-797-5 • Library of Congress Control Number: 2019950931 • Designed by
Frame25 Productions • Printed in Korea through Four Colour Print Group • 15 16 17 18 19 20 XXX 10 9 8 7 6 5 4 3 2 1

For my magnificent Nadia. I wish I had words to
describe the perfection of your many facets and the
extraordinary beauty of everything you are. —S.C.D.

For every magnificent brown girl. You are
marvelous—celebrate yourself every day. —K.J.

MAGNIFICENT
HOMESPUN BROWN

A Celebration

Written by
Samara Cole Doyon

Illustrated by
Kaylani Juanita

TILBURY HOUSE PUBLISHERS, THOMASTON, MAINE

Deep, secret brown.

Like the subtly churning river currents

playfully beckoning me

through my grandmother's kitchen window,

winding steadily past banks of tall grass

and wild rose bushes,

carrying miles of life and endless possibility

on their never-ending journey to the sea.

RO456630441

Deep, secret brown . . . like my eyes.

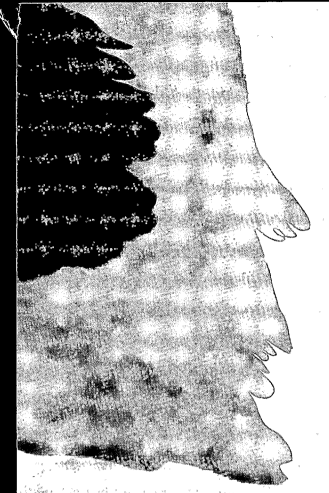

Feathery brown.
Like the jagged shadows
of hemlock branches
thrown over me and Daddy on a gentle
mountain hike.
They pull back periodically to let
sunbeams wash over us in patches,
and slowly grow more enormous than the
towering, tattered triangles
from which they stretch as
the day begins to fade.
We pause every now and then,
saying nothing,
breathing in the full, fresh aroma
and breathing out our worries like an
offering of prayer.

Feathery brown . . . like my lashes.

Amber brown . . . like my hair.

Radiant brown . . . like my skin.

Smooth, creamy brown.

Like the flawless flow of caramel

gloriously smothering my favorite fall fair delight.

Every year I line up with my little brother,

eager to purchase the apple treats from vendors in brightly lit carts

before bouncing off to the midway to watch showhorses pose and prance

while we giddily devour a most ordinary fruit

transformed by the most extraordinarily silky sweetness.

Smooth, creamy brown . . . like my laughter.

Thundering brown.

Like a boisterous, crackling dive

into a mountain of autumn-dried leaves

on my grandpa's lawn.

As my shrieks of joy and triumph shoot to the top of the clear, pale sky,

the last remnants of fragile foliage relent their grip on bare branches

and come tumbling down in defeat.

Thundering brown . . . like my power.

Cozy brown.

Like hot cocoa,

a comfortable cup of liquid dreams

sliding lazily over contented lips,

filling mouths with quiet happiness

as our family gathers to watch the swirling rage of a winter storm,

tucked snugly inside the folds of our giant sofa.

Cozy brown . . . like my peace.

Magnificent, homespun brown.

Like the family tree on Meme's homemade quilt,

forged from fabrics of every shade from creamy,

to amber, to deep secret.

Each inch a poignant memoir,

a personal story, a portrait,

lovingly sewn one into another,

names and dates held together in the form of roots,

trunk, limbs, and leaves.

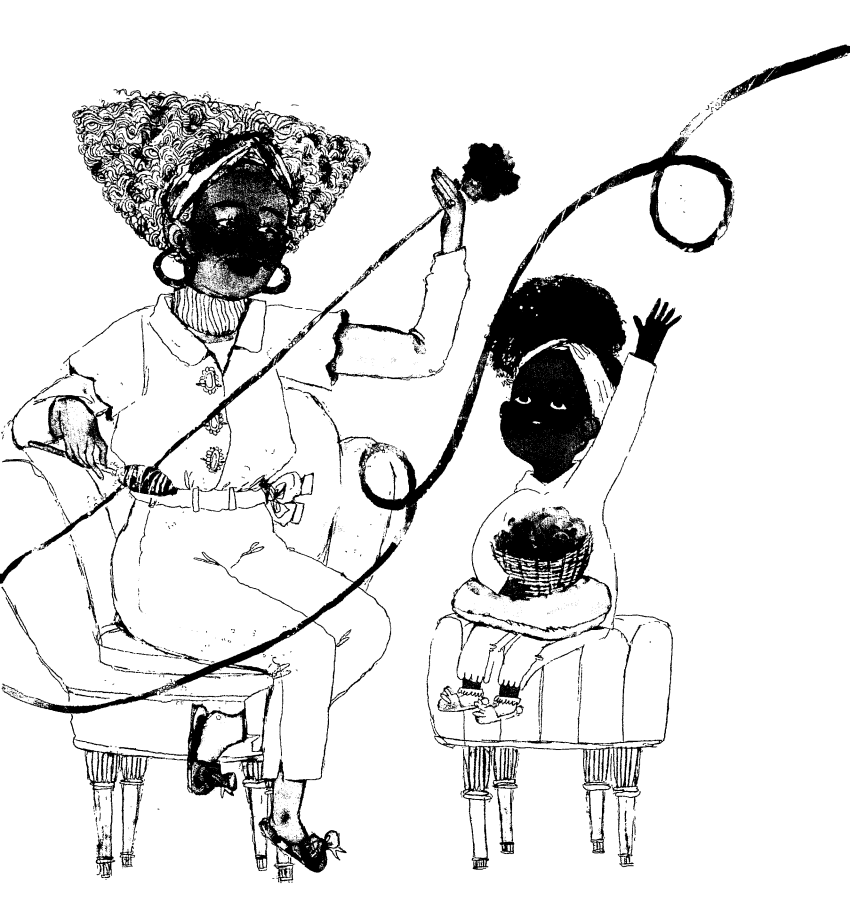

Magnificent, homespun brown,
like all the treasures, places,
and people I love
coming together in me.

A Note from the Author

Thank you for sharing *Magnificent Homespun Brown* with me. This poem began as a deeply personal reflection, a kind of prayer for my own children, and children like them, who are multilayered in their racial/ethnic heritage and sometimes feel as painfully out of place as I once did.

I've been deeply blessed to discover for myself—beyond the stifling boundaries of socially prescribed norms—a firmly rooted sense of belonging through connection to nature and community. Now, with silent thanks, I am watching my children discover it too, among community members who appreciate the blossoming pictures of who they are.

My hope is that we will give all children the chance to embrace and celebrate the many vibrant pieces of themselves, joined together with the same fierce and unrelenting love that sews a cherished family heirloom.

I offer special thanks to Jodi Ferry, an artist whose emphasis on diversity and representation opened my mind to the powerful possibilities of the book this poem could become. And to Kaylani, whose artistic vision and exquisite form brought the message to life most magnificently.

—With gratitude, Samara

Samara Cole Doyon is both a second-generation Haitian American and a deeply rooted Mainer, with half of the roots of her family tree reaching generations deep into the soil of the Pine Tree State. A freelance writer, teacher, wife, and mother, she has been a regular contributor at *Black Girl In Maine Media* and has been featured in the "Deep Water" poetry column of the *Portland Press Herald*.

Kaylani Juanita's mission as an artist is to support the stories of the underrepresented and create new ways for people to imagine themselves. Her work has appeared at the Society of Illustrators and the BBC website, and she is the illustrator of the picture books *Ta-Da!* and the critically acclaimed *When Aidan Became a Brother*. She lives in the Bay Area in California. Look for her online at kaylanijuanita.com and @kaylanijuanita on Twitter and Instagram. Kaylani created the illustrations in this story with digital art, scanned textures, and pencil.